Presented To:

....

From:

....

Date:

....

Keeper
OF THE
Flame

A JOURNEY OF TIME AND SPACE INTO THE HEART,
MIND, & SOUL OF HUMANITY

BY JIM STOVALL

Published by Companion Enterprises, Inc.,
5840 South Memorial Drive, Suite #312,
Tulsa, OK 74145-9082

Companion Enterprises, Inc. books may be purchased in bulk for educational, business, fund raising, or sales promotional use.
For information email jim@jimstovall.com or call 918-627-1000.

Library of Congress Cataloging-in-Publication Data

Stovall, Jim

Keeper of The Flame: A journey of time and space into the heart, mind, and soul of humanity / by Jim Stovall

1. Fiction 2. Personal Growth 3. Inspirational

13 digit ISBN: 978-0-615-22470-1 (Hardcover)
10 digit ISBN: 0-615-22470-9

Printed in the Republic of South Korea

08 09 10 11 12   8 7 6 5 4 3 2 1

Jacket by Judy McHenry – Tulsa, OK
Interior layout / design by Liquid Lotus – Colorado Springs, CO

DEDICATION

This book is dedicated to Dr. Harold Paul,
educator, mentor, and friend
He struck a spark in me that he kindled into a flame
that burns brightly over a quarter of a century later.

About The Author

espite failing eyesight and eventual blindness, Jim Stovall has been a national champion Olympic weight lifter, a successful investment broker and entrepreneur. He is the co-founder and President of the Emmy Award-winning Narrative Television Network, which makes movies and television accessible for our nation's 13 million blind and visually impaired people and their families. The network's programming is also available free-of-charge, 24-hours-a-day at www.NarrativeTV.com

NTN has grown to include over 1,200 cable systems and broadcast stations, reaching over 35 million homes in the United States, and NTN is shown in 11 foreign countries.

Jim Stovall joined the ranks of Walt Disney, Orson Welles, and four United States presidents when he was selected as one of the "Ten Outstanding Young Americans" by the U. S. Junior Chamber of Commerce. He has appeared on "Good Morning America" and CNN, and has been featured in *Forbes* magazine, *Reader's Digest*, *TV Guide* and *Time* magazine.

Jim Stovall has been honored by the President's Committee on Equal Employment Opportunity as the National Entrepreneur of the Year and, in 2000, he joined Bob Hope, Jimmy

Carter, Nancy Reagan, and Mother Teresa when he was recognized as the International Humanitarian of the Year.

He is the author of 12 previous books including *Success Secrets of Super Achievers*, *Today's the Day*, *The Ultimate Life*, and the best-selling *The Ultimate Gift*, which is now a major motion picture from 20th Century Fox, starring James Garner, Brian Dennehy, and Abigail Breslin.

Autographed copies of all of his previous books are available by calling **1-800-801-8184**.

TABLE OF CONTENTS

FOREWORD

My dear reader, as you hold this book in your hands, you have paid me the greatest compliment I can imagine. You honor me by investing your precious time and your hard-earned money in the thoughts, ideas, and concepts contained in these pages. In turn, I wish to compliment you on being a reader and a seeker of knowledge.

As a blind person, myself, I cannot read these words from the written page as you are at this moment. I am embarrassed to say that when I did have my eyesight, I don't know that I ever read a complete book cover to cover. Now, thanks to books on tape and the National Library for the Blind as well as a high-speed tape recorder, I complete—on average—one book each day.

I have read the biographies of over 1,500 great people who have made the world a better place. All of these people, in their own way, exhibit outstanding traits. One of the most common traits among these unique and outstanding individuals is that of being a consistent reader and seeker of knowledge.

You are in fine company.

This book is very different from any of the other books I have written. It is also very different from any of the hundreds of books I have read. I hope it can dispel the myths that lie in two very old sayings. "It's not what you know, it's who you know" and "You have to be in the right place at the right time."

Within the pages you hold, you and I can meet and begin to understand the most important human being you can ever know —which is yourself—and you will be geographically and historically in exactly the right place at the right time.

You and I are about to embark on a journey. It is a journey that will take us around the world, but it will also take us back in time. Learning about other people from other times can act as a mirror to help us understand our own time and place and, more importantly, ourselves.

As you and I complete this journey within these pages, my hope is that this message will accompany you on an even greater journey throughout the remainder of your life. I am privileged to be your traveling companion.

If, as you journey toward your destination, you need a bit of encouragement or counsel, I can be reached at 918-627-1000. I want you to know that from this day forward, you have one person who believes in you and believes in your dreams. If you doubt this, simply pick up the nearest telephone.

I am looking forward to taking this unique journey with you, and I am looking forward to your success.

Today's the day!

—Jim Stovall

CHAPTER ONE
A CHANCE MEETING

There are no accidents on
the road to your destiny.

In the intervening years, I have often lamented, "If I had only known then what I know now." This, of course, is against the natural order of things as it is impossible to avoid a situation using wisdom gained from the very situation one is attempting to avoid. As I put pen to paper, I seek, once and for all, to clear my mind, renew my spirit, and restore my soul.

I looked on as the sun clung like an angry red boil to the western edge of the world. Eventually, it began its slow descent into the sea like an old man settling into a familiar chair.

My journey, as often happens, was ending in the exact, same spot where it began. Although I was in a familiar place, I had become a much different person. Our humanity can only be judged against the backdrop of our life's experience. Too often, we judge people based upon the way they change the world. Instead, we should measure the way the world has changed them.

One of the ironies of this life is that when we most need wisdom born from experience, we are too young to have wisdom, experience, or even the awareness that we are lacking.

It had been 42 years before, in the springtime of the calendar as well as my life. The sun had already set, and I was admiring the dying embers of the western sky. The most brilliant of the stars were just beginning to make their appearance, and the moon stood as a lone sentinel, illuminating the incoming waves where it would preside until the sun made its ritual journey around our world and started the process again by exploding in the east.

I trudged along the water's edge, trying to find that elusive path where the sand is firm enough to hold a walker's weight while still allowing enough distance to keep one's feet dry. Our external world is made up of earth, sea, and sky. Only at the shore do all three come together to create a harmonious symphony.

As I drank in the sights, smells, sounds, and textures, I believed I was fully appreciating my surroundings. I didn't yet realize that the ability to enjoy and experience is in direct proportion to the depth of one's soul.

As a young man, I thought I was appreciating everything and living within the full knowledge of my surroundings. In reality, I was like an art patron trying to experience a masterpiece through a dark and distorted glass.

In the distance, I could just begin to make out a lone figure perched atop an immense rock on a point surrounded by the crashing surf. As I approached, the figure took shape and substance, and appeared to be a tall, gaunt, aged man with flowing white hair and billowing robes. In the gathering darkness and rising mist, it was hard to tell if what I saw was real or simply an apparition.

This is the way of life. Things which appear real, solid, and stable, most often prove to be transient and temporal, while those things that are elusive and indistinct prove to be eternal.

For reasons impossible to explain either then or now, I set my feet on the path that led me out onto the point and toward the mysterious, shrouded figure. As I neared, the soft, indistinct lines took form and solidified. It did, indeed, appear to be a rea person facing out to sea. What I had seen before and would have called an elderly or aged man could more aptly have been described as ancient.

The white, flowing hair streamed out behind him and seemed to have a luminescence of its own like the sea that surrounded us. The black, billowing robes put me in mind of a roiling storm cloud, at once powerful but constantly shifting. Although I was certain that I had approached silently, somehow I knew he was aware of my presence.

He stood like a marble pillar for what could have been a few seconds or a few hours, as we were both trapped in that surreal time and place. Then, slowly, inevitably, he began to turn.

First, I was aware of that profile which, somehow, embodies all of the pain and joy of humanity. As he faced me fully, I was captured then—as now—by those knowing blue eyes that seemed to burn with an eternal flame as old as the universe.

CHAPTER TWO
THE ENIGMA

A flame out of control will

kill and destroy

while one well-tended

will warm all of those

around it and sustain life.

At any moment, I fully expected to rise up from the murky depths of a dream and break through the surface of conscious-ness. But the longer I stood there experiencing the energy of this figure before me, the more I came to realize that while it was nothing like I had ever experienced before, it was not a dream.

In the past, I had tried to take in a sight that defied my ability to fully capture it, or I had heard a combination of sounds that were almost beyond my ability to comprehend, but never had each of my senses been overloaded so far beyond reality all at the same time. It was like the immense power and energy of a volcano that can no longer be contained within the earth.

When I finally gathered enough of my wits about me to begin to register specific details, I became aware that the figure before me was holding a small, earthen jar in front of him in both of his cupped hands. The vessel seemed to shimmer and glow with a light unlike any I had ever known, and although the object was rel-atively small and fragile, he seemed to hold it as if it contained the weight, wealth, and wisdom of the world.

24

He noticed that I was staring at the jar, and that was when he spoke. I couldn't be sure if the voice I heard originated from the throat of the being before me or if it simply emanated from my own mind where it threatened to overpower every sound I had ever heard and everything I had ever known.

In a voice as powerful as the thundering sea around us and yet as precise as an unfolding rose, he spoke asking, "Why have you come here?"

I heard my voice crack and stammer in a hoarse whisper, "I don't know."

He smiled knowingly and said, "They never do."

As I was still staring at the earthen jar he held, he said, "I can see that you are drawn to the Perpetual Flame."

I nodded my head, which was the only response I could manage.

He grasped the lid of the jar with a gnarled hand appearing like a skeleton covered with ancient parchment. As he lifted the lid, the glow from the jar bathed us both in a warm, inviting light.

He spoke as if I were not there, but, instead, as if he were addressing a multitude of pilgrims seeking the secrets of life itself.

"This is the Perpetual Flame. It is, at once, the first and last flame. From this flame, all other flames have come and will come. It is as old as when it was first kindled and as new as a tiny spark struck this very instant."

I stared back into his face, and although I would not have thought it possible, the glow from his eyes intensified as he looked reverently into the tiny, sputtering flame contained in the jar he held before him.

After a long pause, he finally—delicately and lovingly—replaced the lid on top of the jar and resumed his stance with the jar held protectively before him in both hands.

I had a million questions rocketing through my mind, but the one I heard myself ask was, "Who are you?"

I heard him laugh with all of the joy and anticipation of a small child as he replied, "I have been known by a thousand names, but the one that has endured is simply the Keeper of the Flame."

It was my turn to laugh and shake my head. Although I was still experiencing the shock and fear of the situation, the absurdity of my circumstance took over, and I couldn't help but laugh. My reaction didn't seem to surprise or bother him in the least. He simply smiled as if accepting a reality he had already known, and nodded, acknowledging the questions forming on my lips.

In a continuous stream, I blurted out but a few of the inquiries worrying the very soul of my being.

"Who are you, really? Why are you here? Or why am I here? I mean, what are you doing, and how does this affect me?"

He smiled patiently as one explaining the most common, routine facts to a child.

"I am, as I stated clearly, the Keeper of the Flame. I am here because you are here and, conversely, you are here because

I am. Our meeting was as inevitable as the waves that formed halfway across the world that have come together to crash on this rock below us at this precise moment in time."

I felt a strange boldness born of my frustration, fear, and confusion. I blurted out, "I don't have any idea what you're talking about, and you're going to have to do better than that or—"

My statement was interrupted by a rumbling and a shifting in the solid rock below us. It simply divided and opened. One moment I was perched atop immovable granite, and the next, I was falling through the immeasurable void of empty space.

Chapter Three
THE FIRST OF A KIND

*There are none so cold
as those who have felt the
warmth of a flame,
then lost it.*

As I hurtled through space, I was assaulted by a raw fear and, at the same time, an encompassing sense of awe. My mind simply could not register the events that were unfolding around me. I struggled to find a point of reference, but all I registered was the immeasurable, black nothingness of an endless tunnel pulling me straight toward the center of the earth.

Finally, I noticed that the ancient man was descending beside me. He appeared calm and serene as he delicately cradled the earthen jar before him.

At the end of what could have been a few seconds or a few centuries of plummeting through nothingness, I began to experience the sensation of slowing. Finally, I felt our descent come to an end, and the old man and I hovered above an endless, gray mist swirling below us.

My eyes clung to the robed figure at my side. When we were standing together on the immense, solid rock, he had seemed mysterious, forbidding, and frightening, but now, he was my only connection—my only link to everything that I had ever known. Somehow, he sensed my terror and smiled reassuringly.

I looked up, attempting to see where we had come from, but my eyes were greeted with what must have been all the space and darkness that the universe had ever known. No bridge ever built could span the yawning chasm through which we had traveled.

The shifting mist below us seemed to lighten a b t and then the fog parted, revealing a group of huddled figures gathered in a rough circle. They had long, shaggy hair and were clothed in animal skins and foliage. I could hear water dripping and wild animals rustling in the deep forest that surrounded them.

From the edge of the forest, a tall figure emerged and strode confidently toward the center of the gathering. He was wrapped in skins and pelts that hung to the ground. As I continued staring at the figure, totally entranced with what was going on before me, the tall man removed the lid of a small, earthen jar he held before him. A glow emanated from the open jar as a guttural murmur of pleasure and approval rose from the ring of people around the tall man.

He reached down to the ground and picked up a small twig, which he lovingly and delicately put into the flame he held in the jar. He took the burning twig from the jar and placed it upon a pile of brush and logs at his feet. The flame from the small twig licked hungrily at the accumulated brush and logs, and within a few moments, a roaring blaze illuminated the entire scene.

I turned to my robed companion and asked, "Where are we?"

He replied, "The question would be more aptly posed as '*When* are we?' instead of '*Where* are we?'"

My terror and frustration once again swarmed over me, and I blurted out, "Okay, if that's the way you want to be, *when* are we and what are we doing here?"

As the ancient one gazed down at the scene below us, he began to speak. "These are the first among us to capture and keep the flame. They are, indeed, the fathers and mothers of us all. Many generations before these you see here, lightning struck and there was fire. They warmed themselves around the burning trees but did not keep the flame, and it inevitably dwindled away to nothing.

"There have never been people as cold as those first ones to feel the flame and lose it. Rarely does humanity appreciate anything until it is lost and gone. Be it knowledge, beauty, or enlightenment, once someone has tasted from that eternal fountain, he is forever altered and changed. You have heard it said that ignorance is bliss. In a sense, this is true. Once an individual has been elevated, he realizes the depth of the pit in which he dwelt before.

"Then, in the middle of this generation, the lightning kindled another fire, but these people had learned from the previous generations and kept the flame alive. The tall one you see in the center was the first of my kind—the Keeper of the Flame.

"It was many generations before man advanced to a point where fire could be started, so the Keeper of the Flame became the central figure among all of his people. He was honored and protected, more for the flame he held than who he was as an individual. But, through the passage of time, he also became the repository for collected knowledge and wisdom of the day. Because the people knew that the flame and the Keeper of the Flame must be protected at all costs, he was the first source of wisdom, knowledge, and learning.

"Collected knowledge is like the endless accumulation of sand deposited on the shores of time by the ceaseless waves. At a glance, it appears that there is no change or advancement, but over time, millions upon millions of grains of sand endlessly shift and move to develop the landscape. Knowledge builds upon knowledge.

"The thing that differentiates humans from all other life is the ability to share and accumulate the knowledge and wisdom of those who have gone before. Therefore, down through the ages, great men and women can build upon all that is known and has been known without going back to the beginning.

"Visionaries exist only because they are afforded a unique perspective. They see farther than those who have gone before, because they are standing upon the shoulders of giants."

I looked at the robed one beside me and asked, "Why have you brought me here?"

He turned those piercing blue eyes on me and stated, "You have been brought here to observe. What you gain and take away from these observations is the reason for our journey. Life and the passage of time are considered to be the most precious treasures among humans. The only by-product from this passage of time and the thing we call life is collected knowledge and wisdom born out of experience—not only our experience, but the shared and recorded experiences of those who have gone before us."

I said, "Can't you just tell me what it is I'm supposed to learn? Aren't you some type of teacher?"

He replied patiently, "I am but a guide. Experience is the only teacher. Even those who call themselves teachers are nothing more than communicators of their own experience or the collective experience of all of those who have gone before."

As I gazed in wonder at the huddled group of primitive humanity, a million questions rocketed through my consciousness. I was struck by the fact that those figures below me were somehow different, but, at the same time, we were disturbingly alike.

Suddenly, the images below me started to fade as the mist began to close, shutting off our view. Never in my life have I gazed upon anything so seemingly unreal and yet undeniably real.

CHAPTER FOUR
COLLECTIVE LIFE

People who learn to work
and live together
increase one another's
souls.

he blanket of mist spread out endlessly below us, stretching from horizon to horizon. The immeasurable dome of black space hung above us. The only perspective that I could hold on to was the ancient robed figure before me that I knew only as the Keeper of the Flame.

I heard myself ask, "Well, have I learned everything I'm supposed to learn? If so, I guess we can return."

He smiled and spoke to me patiently. "None of us has ever learned all that we are to learn. As we enter into an understanding or gain new knowledge, we also become aware that there is much more to know of which we are still ignorant; therefore, learning becomes an endless cycle forever spiraling upward. The knowledge we have gained allows us to see further into the mist of our own ignorance."

A sense of frustration welled up inside of me and burst forth. "Well, if we can't go back where we came from, and I don't know what it is I'm supposed to learn, how do we go forward?"

He simply stretched out his ancient hand toward the clouds of mist gathered below us. I had been so focused on the Keeper of the Flame, I had failed to notice that the fog below had, once again, parted; but it did not reveal the same primordial scene as before. Instead, I gazed upon a wide, clear river flowing from snowcapped mountains and running through a primitive village.

The village was antediluvian. My eyes and my mind scanned the scene below me trying to find something that I could relate to. While the village seemed contrary to anything I had ever known, there was a certain order or pattern to the life that was playing itself out as I looked on. As the Keeper of the Flame began to speak, the scene below me took on a new focus in my mind.

"Those who you see before you are descendants, many generations removed, from the forest-dwellers you last looked upon. This village and these people have been lost to history. They lived somewhere in the Americas. The exact location and time-frame is not important. Those who later became known as Indians kept these people's memory alive in their oral traditions. The villagers you see below you have always simply been known as 'the old ones who came before.'

"This is the beginning of what you know as civilization— people learning to work and live together within the confines of commonly accepted rules and expectations."

He pointed to the perimeter of the village. He said, "You will notice most of the villagers, both men and women, cultivating the fields. This is an important step in human development. Their collective efforts in growing, gathering, and storing food gave them the first, and maybe the most significant, of human luxuries—free time.

"The forest-dwellers spent all day, every day, simply in a quest to feed themselves. Once a civilization is assured of the most elemental of human needs—being food, water, and shelter—there is free time for people to think, grow, and develop.

"You may have heard it said in one fashion or another that idle hands are a bad thing—somehow referring to the fact that spare time is negative. In reality, spare time is like any other tool. It can be negative, positive, or simply unproductive. Societies advance faster and also become more corrupt in direct proportion to the amount of free time of those populating the society.

"Humanity has a longing to improve its environment. Better food, better clothes, better shelter have always been highly sought after. The most significant investment that can be made by any human being is to invest his time, effort, and energy in improving himself. One's environment or the world as a whole does not improve upon their own. Things do not change without the influence of people. When people change and improve, they automatically change and improve their environment.

"It took many years for the forest dwellers to learn to be cultivators and develop the village you see below you. Although their methods are crude and their dwellings the most primitive ever known, they represent a quantum leap in human development. The forest dwellers sought food, water, and shelter from their environment. These primitive villagers changed their environment to meet their needs.

"What you see below you is the beginning of all human development. It comes as a result of people having free time to think, grow, and develop as they continually seek a better environment and a better life for themselves and their families."

I looked from the village below me into the fathomless eyes of the Keeper of the Flame.

I inquired, "So, I guess everyone who lived at this time had a better life than the forest dwellers."

He stared for a moment into the tiny flame contained within the earthen jar cupped in his hands. He spoke slowly.

"One life is not necessarily better or worse than another. There are different choices and different paths. There are people who have lived for many thousands of years as the forest dwellers did.

"At the time we are seeing now, everyone on earth except those you see below you lived as the forest dwellers you saw before. From time to time, there were even clashes between the two cultures. Humans always have and always will fight anyone and anything that is different or misunderstood.

"Something that is strange or unique somehow threatens the familiar and comfortable. These people in the village have been attacked many times by forest dwellers who inhabit the mountains up the river. Only because the villagers have banded together into a society do they survive.

"In a recent attack on this village by the forest dwellers living in those mountains..." He pointed toward the snow-covered peaks on the horizon. "...a baby was taken captive by the invaders. The villagers tried for many days to scale the mountains you see, but their generations of village living had robbed them of some of the skills that their ancestors possessed.

"Finally, in a last attempt, the strongest men in the village partially scaled one of the mountains to try to recapture the baby. When it became apparent that they had failed again, they prepared to return to their village in final defeat. They resigned themselves to the loss of the baby.

"Then one of them noticed the mother of the kidnapped baby climbing down from the top of the mountain carrying a bundle. All of the village men watched her in awe as she approached them from above. When she finally reached them, they inquired, 'How is it that you were able to scale this mountain when the strongest men of our village failed?'"

The Keeper of the Flame paused and seemed to have a faraway look in his eye. He continued with renewed energy.

"That mother's answer to the village men's question echoes down through the ages. He⁻ simple reply was, 'It wasn't your baby.'

"This points out the eternal relationship between passion and power. We have the ability to do things in which we have an interest. And we are interested in the things in which we have ability."

As I stared at the far, distant mountains covered at their base by dense, seemingly impenetrable forests, I knew I would never forget the lesson of the villagers and, especially, a mother and her baby. I had so many questions and wanted to see much more, but the mists gathered below me, and we, once again, were suspended above an endless sea of clouds.

CHAPTER FIVE
DISTANT WINDS

We are all indebted to the bold ones who seek the far horizon and expand it.

When the clouds next parted, we were suspended above a dark and angry sea. Lightning streaked across the sky, and the thunder could be felt as a deep rumbling in the pit of my stomach. The white-foamed waves stretched to the horizon. They looked like a military procession of evil serpents on a journey to the end of the earth.

As I glanced to my right, I noticed the Keeper of the Flame watching me as I was captivated by the awesome display of power unfolding below us. Then, in one particular y bright flash of lightning, I could see—in the far distance—a shapeless form barely visible where the deadly sea met the angry sky. In subsequent flashes of lightning, the form came closer and revealed itself to be an ancient sailing vessel of some kind.

I was filled with shock and horror, and asked the Keeper of the Flame, "What kind of lunatic would be out in weather like this in a tiny boat like that?"

He smiled broadly and replied, "Very good. Just the question we have come to this time and place to explore."

Faster than the blink of an eye, I was no longer suspended as a disconnected observer far above the scene of violent wind and waves below. I was now standing precariously on the deck of that ancient sailing vessel.

Just a moment before, I would have sworn that I could not have felt more vulnerable than being mysteriously suspended above a place I knew not where at a time I knew not when; however, I would have been wrong. As the tiny craft lurched impossibly down between two mountainous waves, I felt helplessness to a degree I had never felt before and I hope to never feel again.

The small ship, if such it could be called, was made of timbers lashed together with some sort of fibrous ropes. It creaked and groaned in protest as it doggedly began to climb the next wave before us. There were a number of strangely-clad men clambering on the deck around me and in the rigging above me. They were shouting to each other in an unfamiliar tongue. I tried to get one among them to pay attention to me, but it was strangely apparent that I was somehow invisible to them.

I whirled around looking for the Keeper of the Flame, but he was nowhere to be found. He who had seemed so foreign to me just moments ago was now the lifeline that I craved and my contact with everything I had once known.

The next few moments of terror felt like decades. Finally, as will inevitably happen, a slight degree of calmness brought more clarity of the impressions I had of my surroundings. The sailors, if so they could be called, seemed to have an urgency as they went about their tasks, but they did not seem to be panicked.

At what would be called the bow of the vessel, I noticed a larger man with very light skin and long, flowing blonde hair. He had his feet spread wide apart on the deck so as to keep his balance in the turmoil of the violent sea. He did not seem to notice the ocean spray drenching him as he stared out into the endless distance.

As he turned to shout an order to one of the men high up on the mast, I couldn't help but notice he had a gleam in his eye and a smile on his lips. If any man had been created for a time and place, this one had found his home.

The large man I came to think of as the captain continued to shout orders in a foreign tongue. His words had such a sound of strength and confidence, I actually found myself beginning to relax.

As the small boat perched precariously atop still another Herculean wave, a flash of lightning in the distance revealed a dark smudge low on the far horizon before us. I realized, amidst what I had thought to be utter chaos, there was a well thought-out course and a definite plan of action underway.

In what could have been minutes, hours, or days for all I knew, the smudge took form and shape, revealing itself to be a point of land. In a masterful way I would have not thought possible, the captain brought his vessel past the point of land and then deftly turned so that we were instantly sheltered in the relative calm of a bay or inlet. The captain addressed each of his crewmen on the deck in what had to be approval for their performance.

As a strange land rose up on both sides of the small bay, our craft made its way deeper into the shelter that had obviously been our destination all along. As I turned to look back at the violent sea from which we had come, I was instantly once again suspended above this nautical world, and I was once again accompanied by the Keeper of the Flame.

I felt anger toward him, but before I could speak, my curiosity—along with a bit of well-placed fear—overcame my anger.

I asked, "Where are we?"

He smiled patiently and replied, "We are far out to sea at a point unknown by any chart or map of this time. Your sailing companions below us there are stretching the boundary that divides known from unknown."

"Where are they going?" I asked.

He replied patiently but as one having to repeat something just explained, "They are traveling to know that which is not known. Is not all travel that way to a certain extent? The world is divided into three groups of people. There is a large population of those who do not know nor do they care to know of anything outside their mundane, daily environment. Then there are those who wish to know by learning from others who have traveled beyond the bounds of their own knowledge. And, finally, there is a hearty group of souls who will never accept anything less than tasting the salt of an unknown sea while sailing to an unknown land."

"How long ago was this or is this?"

It is hard enough to get used to a strange place without dealing with the unfamiliar element of time. The Keeper of the Flame looked at the small boat now anchored at the mouth of a river that emptied into the bay.

He said, "Those, there, lived and sailed at a time long before any of the explorers with which you are familiar. Thousands of years before Columbus or Magellan, brothers of these you see here set out on incredible voyages with crafts less substantial than the one you experienced. The entire world had been visited by these men or other men like them centuries before the map of the world was completely filled in.

"Some sailors go to gain riches or to be known as the one who went there first. Many others simply undertook a voyage so that they would know what was beyond the known. For these brave souls, knowing became their riches. Experiences became their currency of exchange. They were willing to risk their lives in order to feel and touch and taste all that their world had to offer. But, for this breed of man, there is very little risk, because in their minds, life, itself, lay beyond the next horizon, and anything familiar or comfortable was simply a death of its own making."

The mist closed over the scene below us. I knew I would never forget my brief voyage that would, somehow, take me to my own new world.

CHAPTER SIX

THE ETERNAL BATTLE

Unless one discovers that
which is worth dying for,
he has nothing to live for.

My whole world was once again the endless clouds below me and the impossible void above me. As foreign as this had seemed earlier, somehow it was becoming familiar. I guess that one can grow accustomed to almost anything that is constant and dependable.

The time I had spent thus far with the Keeper of the Flame emboldened me. I turned upon him with more ferocity than I really felt and said, "Look, I don't know who you are or what's going on here, but I have to get some answers out of you right here and now."

The Keeper of the Flame stared at me for an uncomfortable eternity, then his craggy countenance broke into a smile, and he laughed at the absurdity of me making any demands upon him.

When he gained control, as his laughter died away, he wiped a tear from his eye and said, "You have not yet learned that I am but your guide. I could not provide you with answers even if I had them. I am only here to help you find the questions. Any answers that you go away with are answers that you brought with you. You have had the truth all along.

"Knowledge and wisdom come from internal discovery. External forces merely prompt the learning. Mastering one's inner space is the key to mastering the entire universe; therefore, the universe is the only teacher."

I was so captivated by his words, that I failed to notice that the sea of clouds below us had disappeared. They were replaced by an endless plain. A waving ocean of tall grass stretched as far as the eye could see. The sky was a dome of impossible blue, unmarred by any clouds across the entire horizon. The sun blazed down from straight above us. It was a flaming coppery orb that threatened to set the whole world afire.

Far in the distance, I spotted a small procession of men making their way purposefully across the vast plain. As they got closer, I could discern that they were heavily armed with swords and spears and shields. They seemed to be a fearsome band of ancient warriors.

I turned around to try to determine where they might be going and instantly spotted another group of warriors traveling across the plain in such a way that they would meet the first group of warriors at a point directly below me.

The second group of warriors seemed younger, more energetic, and armed with newer weapons. As the first group of warriors arrived below me, it was obvious they were older, and their weapons showed the scars of many battles. Each group formed a semicircle below me, creating a ring of warriors—young and old—in the middle of a vast plain.

The silence was deafening. The unreleased tension was beyond anything I had ever felt.

Eventually, two warriors separated themselves from the ring. One was obviously from the younger group. He was easily the largest and most well-muscled warrior from either group. He had the best weapons and swaggered to the center of the ring with a confidence that only comes from one who knows his superior strength and skill will eventually decide any issue.

The other warrior who approached the center of the ring was probably the oldest one present. His long, flowing gray beard was beginning to turn white. It was obvious that he had been an imposing figure in his day, but time and many battles had taken their toll.

His weapons were battle-worn and could not even be compared to those of the young warrior before him. As the two met in the middle of the ring, time once again stood still.

As the young warrior spoke loudly so all gathered could hear, I was surprised to learn that I could understand his words as they echoed into the distance.

"Well, old man, I never thought you would really face me, or have you simply come here to lay down your weapons and admit that I am the rightful leader of our tribe?"

The fierce old warrior stared at the young giant before him and growled, "I have come to lay down nothing other than a young fool who is not capable of leading his own tongue, much less our people."

The young warrior struck out in anger with what I knew would be a lethal blow of his mighty sword, but t cut through nothing more than thin air. The old warrior, without seeming to move quickly, simply was not there. He was somehow behind the young warrior, attacking his unprotected side with practiced ease and skill.

With a few swift strokes, the old warrior left his huge young opponent lying wounded and bloody on the field of battle. The old warrior stood over his vanquished opponent and spoke to him so all could hear.

"Although I have every right to kill you, I won't do that. Only a fool takes a life when he doesn't have to. There is no honor in defeating one such as you. You could be the leader of our people someday, but you won't win that battle with the strength of your arm or the sharpness of your tongue. That battle can only be won with wisdom born from experience and the love and respect of that which has gone before you.

"If I were to kill you now, I would divide our people; instead, I will ask my young brothers here to join me as we stand together as one against our true enemies."

The ring of warriors below me collapsed into a line which formed behind the old warrior. It began to move away into the distance but halted as the victorious leader directed several of the young warriors to help their fallen comrade. As the line of warriors moved into the distance, I noticed that the Keeper of the Flame was once again standing beside me.

He spoke. "Has it not always been so? Does not the young lion battle the old one before it is time? Eventually, he learns that the real battles are fought and won inside of us.

"There are many things worth fighting for and even worth dying for. True soldiers have known this since the beginning of time, but their strength comes not from the sharpness of their blade but from the rightness of their cause. Life is precious, but if there is nothing worth dying for, there can't be anything worth living for.

"Soldiers know that if you fight, you eventually die. They also know if you don't fight in a just cause, you die anyway. A coward dies a thousand deaths in his own soul. The brave and just warrior dies but once in an honorable battle."

As I gazed into the distance, I realized that the procession of ancient warriors had already disappeared. Below us stretched an endless plain, broken only by a stain of bright red blood representing the lesson we had all learned that day.

Chapter Seven
THE ARTIST

Some create for money
or to please the eye,
but a true artist labors
to touch the hearts
and souls of generations
yet to be born.

n the blink of an eye, I found myself walking along a dusty road, winding through low, barren hills. The Keeper of the Flame trudged along beside me. I was amazed at his pace and ease of movement for one so ancient.

A thousand questions flooded through my being. They had been there since I had met this strange robed figure beside me. I was determined not to voice any of my questions because it seemed that all of my questions directed to the Keeper of the Flame inevitably resulted in still more questions with no answers.

As we skirted another anonymous, low hill in the endless procession that stretched before us, he began to speak.

"You are probably wondering why we are traveling this road and where we are going."

I was determined not to give him the satisfaction of admitting my curiosity. He continued to speak as if I weren't even there.

"Some of the greatest artists the world has ever known lived and worked during the ancient Far Eastern dynasties. The leaders of these dynasties were very powerful but benevolent for the most part. They understood that their responsibility to their people extended beyond defending them from enemies and providing food, clothing, and shelter. These leaders knew that the basic necessities of life merely maintain an existence; but art releases the soul to soar to majestic and unknown heights."

As the Keeper of the Flame continued to speak of the time and place we were entering, I noticed in the distance an ornate, walled city. It sat atop another one of the low hills that dotted this region but, somehow, the terrain was no longer monotonous. The walled city rose like a shimmering beacon in an otherwise unremarkable wasteland.

The gate we approached seemed to be made of bronze. It was intricately carved and displayed an indescribable array of exotic jewels. As we reached the gate, it mysteriously opened without obvious benefit of any human presence. I wasn't sure if it opened because of some hidden counter weight released by an unseen guard on the wall or if it magically opened as just another in the inexplicable happenings that seemed to surround the Keeper of the Flame.

We stepped through the opening, and the immense gate whispered closed behind us. We were in a courtyard surrounded by exotic, low-slung architecture. Each of the buildings was unique and a work of art in-and-of-itself but, somehow, the whole scene of the city fit together like a harmonious symphony.

The Keeper of the Flame turned down a narrow street that was inhabited by craftsmen and merchants. Stalls along the street displayed a magnificent array of intricate handiwork. I could not imagine the skill required to produce these treasures in such an ancient time and place.

As we got farther from the main courtyard where we had entered the city, the merchants' stalls got smaller and the craftsmen appeared somehow more shabby and desperate.

Finally, at the end of the street the Keeper of the Flame led me into a small alley. It was so narrow that much of the sunlight was blocked out. The earthen vessel which held the eternal flame seemed to guide our steps. Finally, we stopped at a tiny opening in the alley where one lone craftsman was working. His concentration was so intense, he was unaware that we had approached and stood before him.

The Keeper of the Flame spoke solemnly with a reverence and respect I had not yet heard from him.

"Before you works the greatest artist of his generation and for many generations to come. His work is incomparable and unparalleled. A thousand years from now, learned people will traverse the globe for a brief glimpse of the work you see before you."

I couldn't help myself as I laughed aloud and blurted out, "If this guy is so great, why does he work in the alley at the farthest point from the courtyard where the popular artists and merchants work? Why is he stuck here all by himself?"

The Keeper of the Flame simply shook his head as someone frustrated with the lack of progress. He sighed and spoke slowly.

"Art cannot be measured by the surroundings of the artist, nor can it be gauged by the immediate popularity of the artist or the artwork. Art can only be valued based upon the contribution it makes to the human spirit and our collective creative souls.

"The master you see before you has been working on that one ivory carving for his entire adult life. It is a series of spheres or globes, one intricately carved inside the other. He is working on the third globe which is inside of two larger ones that were carved by his father and grandfather. His son and his son's sons will work on this same piece for the next century. Only then will this one piece of art be complete. Its greatness will not be understood or recognized for two more centuries, and then the world will proclaim the greatness of he who you see before you."

I looked at the small figure working in front of me and at the ivory carving. I was struck by the fact that the artist was undistinguished and not remarkable in any way, but his artwork was indescribable. My eyes were drawn to the ivory piece like a starving man reaching for a morsel of food. I continued to feast my eyes on the intricate carving being lovingly crafted as I questioned the Keeper of the Flame.

"How is it that those of this time and place cannot see what we see? It should be obvious to anyone that this is a masterpiece."

The ancient one chuckled and said, "It wasn't obvious to you a few moments ago. Nor is it obvious to anyone who judges worth and value based upon temporal surroundings. Those who judge value based upon the image of the artist and not the spirit of the art understand the price of everything but the value of nothing."

As I continued to marvel at the work before me, I asked, "What is this piece worth?"

The Keeper of the Flame sighed once again in seeming frustration and then spoke.

"The piece you see before you is priceless. It cannot be measured in those terms. The master who works here is gladly willing to exchange his life for his small part in creating this piece. His ancestors before him, as well as his children and grandchildren, are willing to make the same trade. They will exchange their entire life's work to be a part of creating this masterpiece."

I continued to gaze at the sight before me, but my view was slowly obscured by the sea of clouds creeping into my vision. Instantly, I was suspended above the endless, now-familiar clouds with the black dome of eternity stretching out above me. Once again, the Keeper of the Flame was next to me. I could not speak. I could only look at him, open-mouthed. The feeling of awe that pervaded my spirit from being in the presence of the master and the masterpiece was inescapable.

The ancient one smiled broadly and nodded. Somehow, he knew that I knew.

CHAPTER EIGHT

THE OLD MAN OF THE
MOUNTAIN

The peaks of life serve as goals,
but—when reached—allow us to view
far distant peaks to come.

When the sea of clouds below us next opened, it revealed a truly awesome sight. It was the first time since I had met the Keeper of the Flame that I gazed upon a sight I knew. Although I had never seen it before in person, I couldn't help but recognize the profile of Mount Everest rising up before us.

I had seen it so many times in photographs, but nothing prepared me for the sheer enormity of the peak that loomed up toward the sky. It may be because Everest is known to be the tallest mountain in the world, or it may be its own majesty, but Mount Everest seems to hold within it a dignity that few images in nature can produce.

I knew that it was a rare day, indeed, when clouds did not obscure the view of the summit, but the time I had spent with the Keeper of the Flame had taught me to expect rare occurrences.

I gazed upon the immense giant that rose up in the distance for what may have been a few moments or a few hours. Finally, I noticed that there was a road below us winding through the foothills toward the base of Everest. Along the barren, dusty track, I spotted a group of young men in long, dark robes trudging up the road toward the mountain. Their path led through winding foothills and skirted around the base of other huge peaks that would have been breathtaking had they not stood in the shadow of the tallest mountain on earth.

As I looked at the young travelers, I asked the Keeper of the Flame my constant question, "What are we doing here?"

He, too, was observing the travelers below us as he replied, "We are here merely to discover why they are here."

The road below us dwindled down to little more than a dirt path. Eventually, it was nothing more than an ancient game trail, traveling through the impossible heights and unbelievable surroundings of the Himalayas. Finally, the path ended abruptly at the precipice of a yawning gorge with an angry river cutting through it far below.

Before I could ask the Keeper of the Flame the logic of a path that goes nowhere, each of the walkers, in turn, calmly stepped off the edge of the cliff and disappeared into thin air. My shock was replaced with surprise when a small ledge was revealed just a few feet below the precipice where the young men had disappeared. They were now traveling along the rock ledge that jutted out from the wall of the gorge.

I observed out loud, "There is no way to see that ledge when you step over the edge of the cliff. They must have known it was there or they wouldn't have jumped."

The Keeper of the Flame replied in a knowing voice, "They had only heard of the ledge's existence. Their faith has enabled them to continue their pilgrimage."

I let out a nervous laugh and heard myself say, "I would have to have more than a rumor or hearsay before I would jump off of a cliff like that."

The Keeper of the Flame thought for a moment and then replied knowingly, "It would depend who told you of the ledge's existence and how badly you wanted to reach the destination at the end of your own pilgrimage."

The ledge wound around a corner of rock, passed under a cascading waterfall, and opened up into a broad, green valley on the other side of the gorge. As the pilgrims continued their journey through the paradise of the fertile valley which was hidden among the tallest peaks on earth, the path, once again, widened and became a well-defined road.

The pilgrims approached a weathered stone dwelling that perched on the edge of a lake that looked like an impossibly blue mirror reflecting the images of the snowcapped peaks all around. As they drew up reverently outside the stone dwelling, an aged man emerged wearing white flowing robes. He faced the pilgrims before him but stared past them into the middle distance. I thought he was staring directly at me until I realized that the eyes the old man directed our way were sightless.

I inquired of the Keeper of the Flame, "Have your pilgrims come all this way to meet an old blind man?"

My guide and companion sighed impatiently and responded, "These pilgrims seek vision, not sight. Their hunger has brought them to the old man of the mountain."

One of the young men separated himself from the group and inquired of the old man of the mountain, "Master, what secrets are you to reveal to us this day?"

The old man directed his empty eyes at the one who had spoken, and responded in a voice filled with serenity and confidence.

"I can only reveal that to you which you are prepared to perceive."

The old man walked down to the edge of the lake and stood before its unbroken surface. He bent and picked up a small stone and threw it into the lake. The stone splashed into the water and disappeared. Circles of tiny wavelets rippled outward from the spot where the stone had splashed.

As the young pilgrims gazed upon the scene, the old man of the mountain spoke. "Every action in this life has a ripple effect. The action you take is a cause. It will create a result which will be the cause of another result, and the circle never ends. Everything is an effect, and is, in turn, effected. We can never escape this."

The old man pointed to the group of young pilgrims before him and directed them, "Each of you, pick up a stone and throw it into the water."

I looked on as six young men glanced at the ground, selected a stone, and moved to the edge of the water. Then, almost in unison, five of the six pilgrims threw their stones into the water. One pilgrim, the one who had spoken to the old man earlier, slipped his stone into a pocket in his robe and smiled knowingly as he turned toward the old man.

The old man motioned the pilgrims to follow him, and he moved toward the entrance of the stone dwelling. He paused in the doorway and turned toward the six young pilgrims.

He spoke. "Today, you have learned cause and effect. Everything has a cause, and everything creates an effect. I asked six students to cast a stone into the water. Five of the six did so, but you…"

A gnarled finger and sightless eyes were pointed toward the pilgrim who had spoken earlier.

"…did not cast your stone into the water."

The young man was dumbfounded. He stood open-mouthed, gazing at the blind man who had discerned his most subtle deception.

Finally, the young man spoke defiantly. "You told us, old man, that there was no way to escape cause and effect, but my stone created no ripples on the water."

The young man reached into his pocket and held a small, smooth stone in the palm of his hand.

The old man smiled an ancient knowing smile and spoke.

"Today I have told you the truth. Every action, every feeling, every thought creates an effect. When you had the thought to defy my instructions, it resulted in an effect which was your decision not to throw the stone, but instead to put it into your pocket. That cause and effect has resulted in the lesson you will learn today.

"The only reality in this world is the thoughts and feelings we each have and how we act upon them. The surface of the water was, therefore, effected by the stones that were thrown, as well as the one that wasn't. In this life, you will live and die based upon how you act and, just as importantly, how you fail to act upon the thoughts, feelings, and beliefs you have.

"Every action taken and every action not taken will effect the world around us; therefore, we gh the consequences carefully, both when you act and when you fail to act."

The old man of the mountain stepped through the door of the stone dwelling and was gone.

The pilgrims stood silently for a few moments and, one by one, moved away back down the road which had brought them to this place.

Eventually, only the young man holding the stone in his hand was left. Finally, he, too, walked away from the dwelling. He moved down to the edge of the lake and gazed out upon its smooth surface. He glanced up once toward the stone dwelling and then threw his stone far out into the water.

The ripples were still moving across the surface as the last young pilgrim walked away.

Chapter Nine
TRANQUILITY

He who would live

in harmony

with everything

and everyone around him,

would know peace, joy, and

lasting happiness.

I knew the image of the old man of the mountain and his message would be with me all the days of my life. Nothing in my experience prior to meeting the Keeper of the Flame had, in any way, prepared me for the odyssey in which I found myself. I was, however, struck by the fact that I was less terrified by the events that were unfolding all around me, and I was more conscious of the meanings within the messages that were being demonstrated to me.

Next I found that the Keeper of the Flame and I were suspended above an endless sea of grass that stretched in all directions. The moon hung low on the horizon bathing the scene in a faint glow. A million stars were displayed like diamonds across an immense velvet pillow.

Below us, a bonfire blazed as the center of the only activity within the immense sea of grass. As I observed the area around the bonfire more closely, I became aware of the fact that there were crude hide-covered dwellings or teepees arranged around the perimeter.

Upon first glance, it appeared that the entire village below was in a deep slumber; but then, upon closer examination, I noticed four sentries posted at well-organized locations around the encampment. The crude dwellings were arranged in a much more orderly fashion than I had first expected, and everything below me seemed almost to be part of nature and the immediate environment. I was aware of an overwhelming sense of orderliness and a sense that everything somehow fit into the natural scheme of things.

The Keeper of the Flame was serenely observing me as I took in the scene below us. He gave me ample time to observe the surroundings before he spoke.

"These people live a life of balance and harmony. They exist in much the same way their ancestors existed a hundred generations before. They do not conquer nature, nor does nature conquer them; instead, these people have become an integral part of the life cycle.

"They give to and take from nature everything that is needed. They go through periods of plenty as well as seasons of drought and deprivation, but they do not understand the concepts of fortune or good luck. They simply know that all seasons and all circumstances have a purpose. They each teach us a lesson, and there is beauty in all life."

As the Keeper of the Flame concluded my introduction to the scene below, I noticed that a hint of light from the false dawn was brightening the scene. As the village below me began to stir to life, a blush of color caressed the eastern sky.

The women of the village were the first to emerge and purposefully went about what seemed to be a morning ritual. They rekindled cooking fires and began preparations for what would obviously be the first meal of the day. Next, some of the younger men appeared and tended to the livestock as they systematically checked various points throughout the encampment to insure all had remained as it should throughout the previous night. Pleasant smells of food being cooked over an open fire reached me as the older men and the young children emerged to greet the new day.

What must have been the entire community gathered around the bonfire and one of the eldest men, dressed in an ornate array of beads and feathers, addressed the gathering in a melodious tongue with which I was not familiar. He then lifted his weathered face to the rising sun, and it was obvious to me that he was giving thanks for all that was about him.

As the village people ate, there was cheerful conversation, and the scene was pleasant and tranquil. After the meal, the children ran and played on the plains as the younger men performed organized labor, and the women cleaned up after the first meal of the day. By midmorning, the children were being instructed by the elders of the tribe, and the women were drying fruits, vegetables, and strips of meat over slow-burning coals. By midday, a group of young men departed on horseback for what was obviously a hunting trip.

The Keeper of the Flame and I observed throughout the rest of the day as the primitive community went through its ritual tasks within what I came to know as an ideal setting.

Late in the afternoon, the hunting party returned. They were greeted by the entire community. Shouts and cheers rose from the encampment, as it was apparent that it had been a good day of hunting.

An evening meal was prepared. Once again, everyone was gathered around the bonfire. Solemn words were spoken, and thanks was given by the elder whom I came to think of as their chief. After the evening meal, young men and women performed ceremonial dances, and elders told stories to the younger people who hung on every word.

Eventually, the village drifted off to sleep, and the Keeper of the Flame and I observed a landscape that appeared just as it had when we first arrived at this time and place.

I was waiting for an explanation of the significance of the day's events.

When it was obvious to me that the Keeper of the Flame was not going to offer an explanation, I inquired, "We have observed these primitive people for an entire day. They do not have any amazing art, remarkable skills, or valuable treasures. As I could not understand their language, I do not know anything of their prayers or lessons. What is it I am to learn here?"

The Keeper of the Flame smiled and seemed to be pleased with my question.

He said, "These people, at the same time, have nothing and everything. Their civilization has not advanced in the way some people would measure it; however, in many important ways, these people do not need to advance, because they already live life in a well-ordered, harmonious, and meaningful fashion. They have everything they need; therefore, they have everything they want.

"They have managed to avoid or overcome a dreadful condition that plagues the minds, hearts, and souls of many people—that is, of course, the lust for more. From the beginning of time, people have fought and died to achieve more money, more land, more power, and more of everything that they think will make them happy.

"This disease of *more* is incurable. It can never be satisfied externally. It is a raging fire that can only be put out when people come to understand that a thing's value must be weighed against how much of life it costs to possess it. People with virtually everything can die on the quest for more, and people with little or nothing can live out all the days of their lives knowing that they have enough. Everything you will ever need has been or will be provided for you."

As I pondered his words, the tranquil scene below us was slowly enveloped in a blanket of clouds. Although the scene had disappeared, the tranquil setting was burned into my mind's eye. I would never forget how a peaceful and unremarkable day could hold within it the treasure which was the knowledge of understanding I would never lack for anything as long as I accepted the fact that I had enough of everything.

Chapter Ten
THE POET AND THE MUSICIAN

Fame cannot feed the

creative soul

It only knows the fulfillment

that comes

from releasing the creation.

The endless sea of clouds engulfed us and became the most dense fog imaginable. The Keeper of the Flame and I were walking on a damp, narrow cobblestone street between dingy buildings on either side of us. The darkness of the night was intensified by the relentless fog.

From what little I could see, I knew we were in a very squalid, rundown section of a large and very old city. From the few voices I could hear passing on the streets and alleys, I suspected we were walking through a city in old England.

The Keeper of the Flame walked silently beside me. I don't know if the flame burned more brightly or if it was simply more apparent in the clawing gloom.

Eventually, we turned down a winding alley and stopped before an open door in a particularly ramshackle dwelling. We stood outside the dwelling and peered through the open doorway into a low-ceilinged room with an earthen floor lit only by a single candle. In the center of the room was a rough-hewn, oaken table, and there was very little else to adorn the bleak setting.

Seated at the table was a shabbily-dressed young man who was writing on parchment with a quill pen. As we observed, he would write for a few moments and then stare into space as he remained motionless for long periods of time.

When I was certain that I had seen all that there was to see in this time and place, I turned to the Keeper of the Flame and uttered, "So?" as my one-word inquiry into the purpose of our visit.

The Keeper of the Flame then told me the name of the young man we were observing. It was the only time during my odyssey that a specific name was revealed to me. It left a powerful impression, because I knew I was looking at what many scholars believe to be the greatest poet of all times. I somehow thought he should be larger than life and ensconced in a palatial setting instead of the humble surroundings where we found ourselves.

A few moments before the Keeper of the Flame had told me the poet's identity, I had been bored. Now, I couldn't help but hear the poet's words in my mind as those same words had gained strength and power as they traveled down through the ages and impacted the world.

I remarked, "I am shocked that someone of his prominence lives and works in this place." I gestured offhandedly at our surroundings.

The Keeper of the Flame gazed around the streets and the depressing dwelling before us as if seeing it all for the first time.

He said, "The prominence you refer to is most often in the historical eye or ear of the beholder. Many times, it does not manifest itself during the life of someone such as the one we visit here. History has forgotten that this creative soul lived, worked, and died where you see him now. The acclaim of his words and his wisdom were not felt by his children or even his grand-children."

I observed the master poet wrestle for words a bit longer. He smiled broadly, folded the parchment placing it in the pocket of his cloak, then rose from his chair and blew out the candle. He walked out of the open door, closing it behind him and proceeded along the alley. The Keeper of the Flame and I followed him for quite a distance through the damp and gloomy night.

Eventually, the poet emerged into a courtyard or plaza in the middle of the city. There were a number of men and women gathered around a raised platform. For a sizable group, it was very silent. There seemed to be a hush of anticipation hanging in the air along with the relentless fog.

The Keeper of the Flame and I stood away from the crowd at the point where the alley emerged into the open area. Eventually, a cheer rose from the crowd as a well-dressed young man stepped onto the platform and waved to the assemblage. He was handed a large harp-like instrument. He then settled himself onto a high stool and arranged the instrument lovingly in his arms.

As his fingers connected with the strings, I knew that the curtain to heaven had opened allowing the ange s' song to escape. As he reverently caressed the harp, the crowd swayed back and forth in rapt attention and unparalleled pleasure.

At the end of each song, gold and silver coins rained onto the platform. The young musician played throughout the night. Eventually the crowd began to disperse by ones and twos, but the musician did not seem to notice his fading aucience. Finally, the Keeper of the Flame and I observec the young musician playing for no one except the poet.

At the end of the next song, the musician smiled and nodded to the poet in recognition. The poet nodded in return and joined the musician on the raised platform. The poet reached his soot-stained fingers into his shabby cloak and withdrew the worn and tattered parchment. He unfolded it carefully and, as the musician began to play with an intensity he had not yet cisplayed, the poet began to read.

"If I am to dream, let me dream magnificently.
Let me dream grand and lofty thoughts and ideals
That are worthy of me and my best efforts.

"If I am to strive, let me strive mightily.
Let me spend myself and my very being
In a quest for that magnificent dream.

"And, if I am to stumble, let me stumble but persevere.

Let me learn, grow, and expand myself to join the battle renewed

—Another day and another day and another day.

"If I am to win, as I must, let me do so with honor, humility,

and gratitude

For those people and things that have made winning possible

And so very sweet.

"For each of us has been given life as an empty plot of ground

With four cornerstones.

These four cornerstones are the ability to dream,

The ability to strive,

The ability to stumble but persevere,

And the ability to win.

"The common man sees his plot of ground as little more

Than a place to sit and ponder the things that will never be.

But the uncommon man sees his plot of ground as a castle,

A cathedral,

A place of learning and healing.

For the uncommon man understands that in these

four cornerstones

The Almighty has given us anything—and everything."

Tears flowed down the musician's face as he let the last strains from his harp fade away into the universe. The poet bowed reverently to the musician and laid the parchment on the platform among all of the musician's gold and silver coins. The poet stepped down from the platform and walked away into the night.

The musician rose and gazed with wonder into the fog where the poet had disappeared. He then lovingly retrieved the parchment and carefully folded it and slipped it into his pocket. He disappeared through an alley on the opposite side of the courtyard, leaving the Keeper of the Flame and me standing alone.

I observed, "The musician left all of his gold and silver coins that he earned for playing here all night."

The Keeper of the Flame responded solemnly, "It is much as if one found the most precious diamond in the world deep within the earth. He would take the diamond away with him and leave the dirt behind."

CHAPTER ELEVEN
WORSHIP OR WARFARE

A Creator Who loves us all

as we are

gave us the capacity

to love everyone

as they are.

The placid, azure sea stretched out below us like a carpet. Its sole interruption was a lush, green island punctuating the mirror-like surface. It stood as a shining emerald sentinel in the midst of the vast blue of sea and sky.

The sun hung in the sky directly above the island, providing its perfect constant of light and warmth. It seemed to be a faultless moment captured in time and space.

As the Keeper of the Flame and I observed the scene below us, somehow our perspective drew closer to the island, and I could begin to discern specific details. The idyllic setting offered profuse green foliage of all sizes and shapes. A riot of colors and textures presented themselves as individual blooms and flowers became apparent.

The island perched majestically on the sea like a lush, green fruit—perfect in every way. It was bisected by a ridge of volcanic mountains and cliffs effectively creating two halves of the world below us.

My guide began to speak. "Many places have been called paradise since the beginning of the world. Much like beauty or value, the concept of paradise rests very much in the eye or mind of the beholder, but few people would argue against this land being an idyllic setting."

As we continued to drift toward the near edge of the island, a village came into view huddled between the magnificent beach and the black cliffs looming up behind the dense forest. A group of people could be seen gathered in a semi-circle around one of the more prominent dwellings within the village.

Everyone's attention drew to a climax as a lone individual emerged from the dwelling. He was dressed in some kind of roughly woven cloth which made up his casual tropical garb; but even with his informal wardrobe, he carried himself with an erect bearing that led us and everyone gathered below to understand that he was their leader.

He smiled warmly and then addressed those assembled before him. "My dear people, we abide in a wonderful land that God has given us. Each morning, the sun rises on the far horizon to warm, light, and nourish our people."

Everyone assembled below automatically looked far out to sea to the point on the horizon where the sun had risen that morning and every morning of their collected lives.

"Our God has shown himself to us through that sunrise which greets every morning and resides with us throughout the day until it disappears over the mountains—at which time we thank God for giving us the morning sun and the day of light and beauty He has provided. All of us have come to worship and understand the one true God in that way. We honor and respect one another for our collective and unerring belief."

The formidable leader paused to consider. He appeared to have a dark storm cloud thrust itself over his countenance as he resumed speaking in a much less loving tone.

"It has come to our attention that there are those who dwell on the other side of our island who are not of our community or our family. They do not honor and respect our God nor do they worship Him in the way we do. We must not allow their pagan thoughts or beliefs to contaminate who we are and what we know to be the one true way; therefore, we will send our best and bravest over the treacherous mountains to confront those who are not a part of us.

"We must commit ourselves and commit our lives to either have those others join us as we worship the one true God through His sunrise and gifts to us, or we must forever vanquish them from our island and from our world."

A disturbing and ominous cheer rose from the group gathered below. Where once there had been a tranquil and idyllic setting, there was now a cold chill pervading everything.

In a miraculous way that I was coming to expect—if not coming to understand—the Keeper of the Flame and I slowly ascended high above the village and toward the formidable, rugged ridge that cleaved this green jewel in the sea.

As we somehow drifted above the highest point of the island, the other half of this paradise came into view. It seemed almost identical to the setting we had just experienced. The sun still hung directly above the ridge. There was a covering of deep green foliage below us, and at the edge of the sea, a sandy beach punctuated the separation between sea and land.

Another village was evident among the trees and spilling onto the beach. The inhabitants circled what I came to think of as a council fire as their leader slowly walked around the circular edge of the crowd so that he could face everyone in turn.

He was a squat, powerful man with an air of confidence that had a bit of a violent edge. His words rang out for all to hear and certainly obey.

"We cannot allow those infidels beyond the mountains to threaten our faith or dishonor our God. We know that God is with us in the only way He has ever been with us and will, forevermore, love and honor our people.

"Every day in the middle of our labors, the sun appears over the mountain peaks to remind us that God approves of the work we have done throughout the morning, and He will remain with us until the end of the day. We all gather to worship the one true God as the sun with which He has honored us sinks into the sea as a benediction to the gifts God has given us and the love that He has for us—his true and worshipful people."

The circle of humanity seemed to be drawn to his words like the vortex of a whirlpool. They collectively gathered energy as they focused even more intently on their leader. His words took on a tone that indicated an even stronger conviction that would not and could not be opposed or even argued.

"Before our God who is with us at the end of each day, and whom we worship in the artistry and magnificence of His sunset, we will eliminate those who blaspheme Him by their very thoughts and words that there is another God."

The Keeper of the Flame and I rose high above the village and toward the peaks that separated the two parts of this world. When we reached the summit, I found myself standing next to him atop the highest point of land in this island world.

If I looked to my right, I could see soldiers moving toward me from the village that worshipped the sunrise. To my left I could hear the angry shouts and battle cries from those who found their God in the sunset. I turned and spoke to the Keeper of the Flame who stood as a statue before me.

"I cannot believe what I have seen here. These people live in paradise, and they are preparing to destroy everything they have and kill one another simply because they experience the sun from a different perspective. This is the most insane thing I have ever seen."

The Keeper of the Flame solemnly looked to his right and to his left, taking in all that I had witnessed. He began to speak.

"Insanity, indeed, but it is in no way unusual or unique. Sadly, the scene that is playing out before you has been commonplace and ordinary since the beginning of time. From his earliest moments on earth, man has understood that this fabulous creation must have a Creator. They have further understood that this Creator must love and honor all of humanity, because He has given us everything. We are drawn to Him with our desire to relate to Him and worship Him for all that He has meant to us."

The Keeper of the Flame's expression saddened, and his eyes gazed at a point of rock a few feet from where we stood.

"Sadly, more wars have been fought, blood shed, and dreams dashed on the cruel rocks of hatred in the name of a loving and compassionate God. Both of these tribes worship their God in the way they know and understand and in the way He comes to them each day. They do not understand that the same God comes to their brothers and sisters on the other side of the island in a slightly different time and manner each day as well

"The tragedy occurs when people take their eyes off of the God they love and worship, and begin to love and worship their beliefs and traditions. When one simply loves God and everything He has given us, there remains no room for any prejudice or hatred in the world. When one loves his own perspective or tradition,

KEEPER OF THE FLAME

everything that contradicts that becomes hateful, and the world and God's love shrinks into an evil struggle."

As I looked at what I thought had been a unique and unusual event unfolding below us, I realized that this was the ongoing struggle in a terrible fight as a part of an evil battle in an insane and ongoing war that had existed from the beginning of recorded history.

My guide and companion spoke. "That which has always existed in the past does not have to necessarily represent the future; but the future will not change on the battlefield. It will change—if it ever does—in the hearts, minds, and spirits of loving men and women seeking to worship their Creator and love all of those around them who are a part of His creation.

CHAPTER TWELVE

THE INTERSECTION OF THE WORLD

All people can come together at the table of learning and knowledge.

My fantastic travels in time and space with the Keeper of the Flame were teaching me many lessons. In fact, they were changing me from the inside out. I came to realize that to possess knowledge without being changed is to not really possess the knowledge at all.

I was also struck by the fact that the mysterious way in which we moved through the miles and centuries was becoming less incredible to me with each journey. I guess that one can grow accustomed to almost anything. We can take miracles for granted if they happen often enough.

The heat was oppressive, beyond anything I had ever known before. The sun reflected torturously from the endless miles of sand.

The Keeper of the Flame and I were trudging along a dusty road in the midst of a long line of travelers. These travelers represented perhaps the oddest assortment of humanity I had ever seen gathered in one place and time. There were wealthy sultans with

all of their attendants. The incredible value and rarity of their possessions would dazzle the richest king. There we e merchants with
all manner of goods and crafts from the corners of the globe. There
were scholars, theologians, soldiers, and others who had simply
banded together for ease and safety of travel.

The Keeper of the Flame was explaining all of this to me as
we slowly crept across the burning desert.

Finally, in desperation, I asked, "How much farther do we
have to go?"

The Keeper of the Flame laughed softly and replied, "Any
journey becomes bearable when one knows and understands its
end. We will reach our destination in the cool of the evening."

At that point in time, I had greater anticipation of the cool
of the evening than wherever our destination might be. The Keeper
of the Flame, I noticed, seemed little effected by the oppressive
heat and rigorous travel, particularly for someone of his obviously
advanced years.

He spoke as if he had not a care, a concern, or the least
discomfort. "These caravans traversed the known world during
this time and in this place. They served not only to spread products,
crafts, and goods to people who had never had access to these
things, but these caravans also collected and delivered the most
precious commodity in the world. They spread the accumulated
knowledge of their time.

"These people respected wealth, strength, power, and beauty, but they revered knowledge and learning beyond anything else. They realized that knowledge is the key to understanding, and understanding is the key to acceptance. Acceptance is the key to harmony, and harmony is the key to peace and love. People from diverse backgrounds and beliefs can live in peace and love given enough knowledge and understanding."

Finally, the dusty road we traveled ended at a great walled city. It was an oasis in the desert. All manner of exotic fruits, vegetables, and animals were on display as we made our way through the streets.

At what proved to be the end of our journey, we drew up at the edge of a massive bazaar. There were booths displaying every conceivable item in the world. As the Keeper of the Flame and I made our way around the edge of the bazaar, I noticed a second then a third road that entered the bazaar from different points of the compass.

The Keeper of the Flame explained, "This place is the crossroads of the known world. Three great trade routes come together at this one point. The first people to travel to Europe, Africa, and Asia all came through this crossroads. Far more valuable than their exchange of goods was their exchange of knowledge.

"The word you know as *trivial* or *trivia* comes from this time and place. Tri for three. Via for roads or routes. Where the three great roads came together, people would exchange facts, details, and news of the day. This network of information became known as *trivia*.

"The greatest library yet known in the world was established in this place. It became the repository for the collective knowledge of the greatest scholars of the entire known world. People would travel literally for years to make their way to this spot to gain knowledge and, even more importantly, to present the knowledge they had gained from their lands and from their travels to this place.

"It has been said that there was knowledge stored here that has never been duplicated or equaled even in the ensuing centuries. Humanity will never know, because the great library at the crossroads was destroyed by an ignorant and evil ruler just a few years after this time we are experiencing here and now. When the knowledge in the library and, more importantly, when the exchange of learning was eliminated, humankind was set back many centuries.

"The splendid colors and plumage of the brightest bird fades into darkness when the candle is extinguished. The knowledge still existed in the minds of some scholars, but it was no longer stored, collected, and exchanged, so it eventually faded away.

"Knowledge is built upon knowledge. Humanity is separated from all other creatures in that human beings can exchange knowledge with one another so that one person may learn from the experiences of literally hundreds who have gone before."

The Keeper of the Flame and I arrived at the steps of the most massive building I had ever seen before or since. A wide set of stairs marched majestically up to massive columns that seemed to be holding up the heavens above. Eventually, we reached the top step and turned to look back across the entire city far below.

The Keeper of the Flame spoke. "As it is here, it should be everywhere—that the seat of knowledge, understanding, and learning presides far above all other human endeavors below."

After we had gazed at the activity and commerce below us for a time, the Keeper of the Flame turned and led me toward massive doors that were opened upon our approach by huge uniformed guards who protected the entrance to the great library. As we entered, the breath left my body, and I stood in amazement gazing across untold ranks of parchments, scrolls, tablets, and every manner of material that could conceivably record and display knowledge and learning.

Hundreds of robed figures shuffled their sandaled feet across the marble floor, lovingly tending to each volume in the great library. Thousands of scholars representing every race, color, and creed on earth were seated in small cubicles around the perimeter, hungrily devouring the feast of learning that was so plentiful.

Finally, the Keeper of the Flame led me back through the massive doors and down the myriad of steps to the street below. He turned to look back at the great library and spoke.

"This place was eventually destroyed because of the fear of one ignorant ruler. He believed that if the people gained enough knowledge, somehow he would lose his power. He was wrong. Knowledge should never be feared. It is always the first step to understanding and acceptance. Ignorance shou d be feared as it is the first step to confusion, misunderstanding, bigotry, and hatred.

"He who would have peace and tranquility must first embrace knowledge and learning. We fear that which we do not know. We can only love that which we intimately know and understand."

CHAPTER THIRTEEN

STEPPING THROUGH THE DOOR OF ENLIGHTENMENT

Only when all knowledge is available to all people can we each reach our destiny.

As the Keeper of the Flame and I walked away from the massive library in the great city at the crossroads of the known world, I was deeply moved. I stopped several times to gaze back at the unbelievable sight of the ancient library holding all of the accumulated and recorded knowledge of the day. It was hard to imagine that it was to be destroyed, and much of the wisdom and learning was to be lost forever.

In many ways, we have advanced as a people throughout the years, and in other really important ways, we remain much the same.

As we walked along the dusty road, we left the crossroads farther and farther behind. Eventually, the road was covered by a wall of clouds, but the Keeper of the Flame seemed unaffected, and we walked on, guided by the light emanating from the earthen vessel he held before him.

As we eventually emerged from the curtain of clouds, I somehow knew that we were in a totally different time and place.

The landscape had changed. It was much steeper, and the hills and valleys were covered with lush green foliage. The air was crisp, well into the fall of the year with a hint of winter all about.

We passed through dense forests and emerged to walk among fertile fields which had already been harvested for the year. Eventually, the road wound through mountainous terrain with snow-covered peaks foretelling of the barren season to come. Finally, we drew up before a small village below us, nestled in a valley surrounded by impossibly-steep and towering peaks.

The Keeper of the Flame spoke. "Many centuries after the devastating loss of the great library, there was a monumental development that made it impossible for any evil or narrow-minded person to ever totally destroy wisdom and learning again. Before the time and place we are visiting, the learner or student had to travel to a teacher or source of wisdom and knowledge. Then, one day, the world changed and can never be the same again."

The Keeper of the Flame led me through a small village, and we drew up in front of a weathered workshop with an open door revealing workbenches and low tables covered with a confusion of tools, metal parts, spare pieces, and an assortment of indescribable items. There was a lone figure wearing a leather apron seated at the workbench, laboring over several small pieces of metal. I couldn't imagine what monumental impact could come from such a modest setting.

The Keeper of the Flame once again spoke. "From this point in time forward, learning, information, communication, and wisdom began to be available to all people, everywhere. What you see before you is the birth of the printing press. It made it possible for thoughts to be reduced to paper and readily distributed throughout the world. Books and printed material were scarce for several more centuries, but the bonfire of enlightenment was kindled by a tiny spark struck in this very place."

We looked on as pieces were assembled and tested. Darkness closed in over the village, but the figure before us lit a lantern and worked far into the night. Sometime before dawn, he drew a piece of pressed parchment from a small drawer in the workbench. He lovingly rolled it into the machine and after several minutes, what emerged was a crudely-printed page. The craftsman continued to delicately make adjustments to his creation, and the pages that emerged continued to improve.

The Keeper of the Flame explained, "Centuries from now, single pages printed in this obscure place will sell for a king's ransom—not because of the words on the page, but because of what the page, itself, represents. Make no mistake, there will always be those narrow-minded people who will try to destroy the thoughts, hopes, and dreams of others by burning or banning books, but once that magnificent bell in the steeple tower of wisdom and freedom rung, that sound could never be stopped.

"Words communicate our thoughts and feelings. Although they are often inadequate and fail us, they are all we have to share the best parts of ourselves with one another. From this point forward, words became the property of all the people.

"Printing was improved immeasurably, and, eventually, words were sent around the world without the need for paper or ink. There will continue to be developments in the delivery and communication of thoughts and ideas, but this humble printing press represents a fork in the road for humanity that will alter this one's sons and daughters forever."

The sun was peeking between two of the snow-covered summits signaling the beginning of a new day. I realized that it would be many decades and centuries before history would even begin to understand the significance of this new day that was dawning. I would forever be changed by this experience, and I would never again hold a book in my hands without thinking of the night that the printed word was born.

CHAPTER FOURTEEN

THE MARATHON OF LIFE

The ultimate race is always
run within the human mind.

The Keeper of the Flame and I next stepped from the sea of clouds onto a dusty road traversing a fertile plain with groves of olive trees all around us. There was a sense of planning and order about everything in this time and place. We emerged from the olive groves atop a slight rise in the landscape that afforded a view of a great city gleaming in the distance. Instantly, I knew where we were.

The Acropolis and the other majestic marble structures were familiar to me; but instead of looking at the remnants of a great civilization on a postcard, I found myself looking upon a bustling city in the midst of a thriving civilization.

As the road took us closer to Athens, the Keeper of the Flame spoke. "The Greeks of this time and place will always be known for the myriad of gifts they gave the world. They were, above all, thinkers, in every sense of the word. They were men and women of thoughts and ideas. Much of art, theatre, higher learning, medicine, and philosophy were born here and now."

As I gazed in rapt attention at the foreign but yet familiar surroundings, I asked the Keeper of the Flame one of the vast number of questions pressing upon my mind.

"So, is it art, theatre, higher learning, medicine, or philosophy that we have come to observe?"

The Keeper of the Flame replied solemnly, "We have come to observe an important slice of life impacting none of those developments directly but all of them indirectly."

Once again, the Keeper of the Flame had answered one of my inquiries, leaving me with more questions than before.

We wound through the ornate and orderly streets of the city. Commerce, human discourse, and lofty conversation were all about us.

Finally, we arrived at a great stadium crowded with anxious spectators. There were, obviously, people from many foreign lands in the assemblage. An oval track ringed the inner edge of the arena, and chants and cheers rose from sections of the stadium as various athletes wandered onto the track. The athletes of all shapes, sizes, and colors—and speaking diverse languages—greeted one another as they converged in front of a stately official mounted on a podium along the inner edge of the track.

The official began to speak in a commanding tone so all in the vicinity could hear. "We have gathered today for the great race. The marathon represents the ultimate challenge for any competitor. You have come from all corners of the known world, representing your countries, your people, and—most important-ly—yourselves.

"It is vital that each of you compete well this day. Competing well not only consists of how you run the race, but, maybe more importantly, it consists of how the race runs you. You must win or lose with honor, dignity, and sportsmanship worthy of the people and the countries you represent.

"If this competition is only about who may cross the finish line first, there can be but one winner; but if these games are to bring about the best in each of us, there will be one champion, and the rest will each be winners."

The various athletes were introduced in turn and saluted their section of the cheering crowd. The biggest cheer rose when the runner representing Greece, itself, was introduced. He was a marvelous specimen of humanity. His physique put me in mind of an immense marble statue, perfect in every way.

Each of the other competitors was ntroduced in turn, and the final athlete was then presented to the crowd. He was a small, dark-skinned man and was competing to represent what was a little known part of northern Africa. No cheer arose as he took his place at the starting line. Obviously, none of his countrymen had traveled the great distance to the games in Athens. A polite smattering of applause was offered up from the other spectators in the arena.

The official explained that the marathon would consist of one lap in the stadium and then the competitors would run a 26-mile course that had already been laid out throughout the countryside, and, finally, they would conclude the race with one final lap in the stadium.

Each of the competitors arranged themselves on the starting line. They were all dressed colorfully and with great care. The obvious exception was the African who was attired in worn animal skins and had no shoes on his feet.

At a signal from the official, the race began, and a deafening roar rose within the stadium. The Greek runner proved to run as well as he appeared he would. He was well in the lead at the first turn, and each of the other competitors jostled for position behind him. As he lengthened his lead on the backstretch, I couldn't help but notice that the African runner had already fallen far behind and seemed not to be caught up in all of the excitement surrounding the event. He seemed oblivious to the roaring crowd and the excitement of the moment.

The Greek runner was first to leave the stadium and begin the course that wound through the countryside. A cheer rose as each of the competitors departed through the massive gates. I couldn't help but feel a twinge of embarrassment as the African runner was the only competitor in sight as he finally reached the gate and left the stadium.

The crowd settled itself, and other events of the competition were held on the track as everyone anxiously awaited the return of the runners and the final lap of the marathon race.

Several hours later, a messenger rushed into the stadium and approached the official who was perched atop the podium. He handed a message to the official who immediately announced that the marathon competitors were approaching the stadium for the conclusion of the great race.

A roar of anticipation rose from the massive crowd. All eyes were riveted on the open gates at the end of the stadium that beckoned the athletes toward the finish line.

The roar of the crowd was instantly extinguished and a stunned silence fell as the small, barefoot African was the first to enter the stadium. He ran awkwardly around the track and finished the race as the other competitors, one by one, entered the great stadium.

As I stood in shocked amazement, the Keeper of the Flame answered the unspoken question that loomed before everyone present.

"From the beginning of time, observers have wondered why certain competitors win and others do not. If the race always went to the competitor who appeared most qualified, there would be no reason to compete. The purpose of competition is not to learn about outward results, but inward resolve.

"The Greek runner and many of the other competitors are among the most gifted athletes of their time. They have trained and competed all of their lives. They have soaked in the adulation of a thousand crowds and have run for glory and honor.

"The African comes from a proud people who run as a way of life. They do not compete in races but run great distances as a rite of passage to adulthood. Casual observers thought that the African had no chance because he was so far behind after the initial lap around the stadium.

"The other competitors ran for the glory and the sound of the cheering crowd, but once they left the stadium, much of their motivation left them. Then, for several hours across the hot and dusty plains and through the foothills, the African did what all great competitors do. He represented his people by running for himself.

"Every race and, indeed, every competition is won or lost in the mind of the competitor. The competition merely reveals the character of the runner. The victory is little more than an outward confirmation of the greatness within."

The official motioned for the African to run a victory lap around the stadium. His fellow competitors lined the track and cheered as he passed. The crowd rose as one and applauded the diminutive runner who had taught us all a great lesson about marathon running and life.

CHAPTER FIFTEEN
KINDRED SPIRITS

*One can find reverence
and respect in every part
of creation.*

The sea of clouds once again extended to infinity. The Keeper of the Flame and I were suspended in what I came to think of as a transitional place in time and space. I was becoming more accustomed to the surreal happenings during my time with the Keeper of the Flame.

I did not understand how or why things and events were unfolding the way they were, but I realized that I had come from a world of technology where I understood very little of how everyday, common things worked. In my finite mind, the travels in time and space with my guide were becoming no more or less miraculous than flipping on a light switch or speaking instantaneously via a telephone to someone halfway around the world.

The sea of clouds began to slowly dissolve like a curtain of filmy gauze haltingly being drawn back to reveal that which is beneath. My first glimpse of the landscape below me caused my heart to race and the breath to be caught in my throat. The incredible vista that stretched out below us was a banquet for the senses.

There were mountains that were rugged and majestic, powerfully stretching toward the impossibly-blue sky. There were rushing streams of white water that cascaded down from the peaks anxiously seeking the security of lower elevations. There were forests of pine, fir, and birch trees that marched in rank up the sides of the peaks, dwindling away at the timberline. All manner of wildlife was in evidence, seeming to know that they fit into the wilderness as a part of the natural order of things.

The Keeper of the Flame spoke. "Since the beginning of time, man's best efforts to improve his environment have been little more than futile gestures. The most magnificent structures built by men and women pale in comparison to the cathedral that nature has crafted. Society has tried to conquer nature and, in many cases, it has done little more than dilute or even diminish it.

"Nature is like a beautiful symphony. One can appreciate it or play in harmony with it. To try to alter it is to subject the master's handiwork to the most crude form of graffiti."

As I drank in the impossible scene of beauty below us, I noticed a lone figure traveling along a mountain stream. He had long, flowing hair and a shaggy beard. He was dressed from head to toe in animal furs and skins. He carried a long walking staff and a very old flintlock rifle. All of his possessions were carried in a crude pack slung over his shoulder.

Like the wildlife, he seemed to be more a part of the scene than someone traveling through it. He gave the impression of casually moving along in a random fashion, but, somehow, I knew that he was taking in all of the sights, sounds, smells, and textures around him.

He walked along the stream and paused at the point where it converged with a larger river. He reached into his pack and unrolled a tanned animal hide to reveal a crude map. With a piece of charcoal, he made several marks on the hide, then he lovingly rolled it up and placed it back in his pack.

The Keeper of the Flame spoke. "This is the first of his kind to experience this place. Others have gone before, but they left no mark on the land nor did they map or record their travels. This one is the earliest of what later became known as the mountain men. They were a rare breed of brave souls who went into new and strange lands and lit the light that pushed the darkness back, extending the horizon for the less bold ones who would come later."

We observed the mountain man moving through the wilderness throughout the day. He traveled swiftly and silently, leaving no trace of his passing.

Late in the day, as darkness was descending quickly on the mountainous terrain, the mountain man knelt to observe some animal tracks that crossed his path. The tracks were impossibly large and spaced in such a way that it could only be a massive grizzly bear. The mountain man followed the tracks and moved through a jumble of boulders strewn at the base of a mountain. He emerged before a placid stream flowing down from the peaks. In the middle of the stream, a giant of a grizzly bear was calmly eating his fill of fish that he was deftly catching with his immense paws. The grizzly displayed a grace and quickness unexpected in a beast of his size.

The mountain man crept closer, removed his pack, and raised his rifle to his shoulder. At that point, natural instinct took over, and the bear turned toward the mountain man, somehow sensing his presence. The bear instantly rose up on his back legs to defend himself. The bear and the man stood frozen in time and simply looked at one another. Fear, mixed with respect and awe, passed between them. Eventually, the mountain man lowered his rifle and slowly backed away. The bear lowered himself, crossed the stream, and moved into the trees on the opposite bank.

The Keeper of the Flame spoke. "Both the man and the bear are the most dominant and imposing figures of their kind. When they met, they recognized that about one another. Somehow neither had the desire to diminish the wilderness by eliminating the other.

"The natural order of things is the survival of the fittest. The weak perish so that the strong may live, but when two with the most strength meet, it is often enough to recognize one another and allow nature to continue in an act of reverence and respect."

My companion and I somehow rose far above the land-scape, and as I was observing the beauty below me, in the blink of an eye, it changed.

The Keeper of the Flame continued, "It is now years later. He who came first has been followed by those who can only follow when someone has broken the trail. Then those came who would settle here and change the landscape forever. It is one of the great ironies of nature that for any more than a handful to enjoy the most beautiful settings, somehow the setting they came to enjoy must be diminished.

"Those who would be comfortable or those who would settle are to never know the exhilaration of being the first to view a peak or walk a mountain valley."

Below us now were well-defined trails. Some might even be called rutted roads. Covered wagons in long snake-like processions made their way through the mountains. A few log cabins dotted the landscape, and, at the intersections of rivers or the converging of roads, there were small settlements.

The Keeper of the Flame once again spoke. "The many cannot live as the few do. These have come to build a better land and a better life for their children and grandchildren. In some ways, it is better, and, in other ways, it will never be what it once was. The bold one who came first and his brother mountain men who followed him have moved farther and farther back into the wilderness, always seeking a new horizon."

The Keeper of the Flame and I were suspended far above the mountains. We moved farther and farther away from the roads, the log cabins, and the humble settlements. Eventually, the terrain became even more rugged. There was an impossibly-deep gorge with a foaming white river racing through it. A huge stone promontory jutted out defiantly hundreds of feet above the raging river.

There was a lone figure seated on a boulder atop the promontory. He had long, white hair and a beard to match. He was dressed head-to-toe in well-worn skins and furs. The rifle propped up beside him had been well-used as it had fed him for many years; but the rifle, like the old man, still appeared formidable. He enjoyed the scene of beauty from atop the promontory until the light of day began to fade. Eventually he rose and moved down the mountain toward the tree line.

As he rounded a point of rocks, instantly a huge bear loomed up in the path before him. It stood on its hind legs, ready to defend itself from anything or anyone. I knew there could not be two bears the size of this one. The grizzly had white hair flecked throughout its fur. He bore the scars of many battles, but stood defiantly in the path. Time stood still as the old man and the bear, once again, confronted one another.

The old mountain man spoke. "So, we meet again. I can see that you have lived well, as I have. We are a dying breed that was only made for a certain time and place. Our time has almost run out, but, if you're agreeable, we will both go our own way—once again—to see, smell, and taste that which is left for us before we pass on."

The two giants stared at one another. Somehow, in their own way, they communicated. Eventually, the bear ponderously lowered itself to all fours and walked away. The mountain man watched the bear moving into the distance. The bear turned to look at the man one last time before he disappeared into the trees.

As the clouds closed over the pristine beauty below us, the Keeper of the Flame spoke. "These mountains will always be among the most beautiful places on earth, but no one will ever know these mountains like the two great spirits you met today. They recognized the beauty and majesty in nature as well as the significance of one another."

CHAPTER SIXTEEN
A HUNGER FOR LEARNING

*The quest for knowledge
is a journey that is never
completed.*

When next the great sea of clouds dissolved, a bustling, ancient city was revealed. Bronze-skinned people were going about their daily lives within the thriving community. As I tried to take in the scene below, the Keeper of the Flame began to speak.

"This is the Indus Valley—or what you would know as India. We have arrived approximately 4,000 years before the time you know. This civilization is well-developed and far-advanced for its time and place. The city was built on straight streets that were obviously laid out in a pattern. The inhabitants live in one or two-story houses made of baked bricks. Each home has its own well, and clay pipes remove the sewage to a central location. These people were very artistic and were skilled craftsmen working with gold and silver.

"This city was built very quickly and shows a prior knowledge of architecture and construction. These people had a hunger for learning that made them more developed than the generations that would come after them."

The Keeper of the Flame and I were walking on one of the many streets through the orderly community. I was taking in all of the sights, sounds, and smells of this fascinating time and place.

It was hard for me to realize that, while these people lived 4,000 years before the time that I think of as the present, their civilization was much like what I know.

The flow of pedestrian traffic seemed to be all converging into a main street and moving in the same direction. The Keeper of the Flame and I fell into the flow of traffic and walked toward the edge of the city. The procession of humanity passed through the city gates and wound through cultivated fields and well-tended herds of cattle. I continued to marvel at the state of development that existed 4,000 years ago.

I found myself trying to understand what elements had come together to make these people so advanced at such an early time in history.

Eventually, the procession arrived at a huge field, and the people began arranging themselves around a low platform at one end of the open area. Everyone seemed excited, and a sense of great anticipation fell over the crowd for whatever they had come to experience. Although there were many hundreds of people arranged across the open field, everyone was very well behaved and almost reverent as they awaited the beginning of the event they had come to witness.

Eventually, a tall, thin man with a white beard moved slowly but confidently to the platform. The lines in his face bore the evidence of many years of life. A hush of anticipation fell over the crowd. The sense of respect and reverence for this man was like a tangible, living thing that moved across the open field.

The old man stepped to the edge of the stage and looked across the sea of faces. He seemed to establish genuine eye contact with everyone, although I knew that would not be possible. He began to speak in a voice that managed to be loving, commanding, and knowing—all at the same time.

"Today, I want to speak about the valuable things of this world. Anything that can be bought or sold, and anything that can be replaced, is of minimal value. All the gold in our fair city cannot buy one minute of the sunshine we are all enjoying or the fresh air we are breathing or even the companionship and love of those around us.

"People know the cost of everything and the real value of nothing. Who among us, upon his deathbed, would not give all he possessed for one more day of life on this earth? While this is true, most of us have wasted many days of our lives in an attempt to obtain possessions that really don't bring us peace, happiness, or joy. This is not to say that the possessions of this life have no value at all. They buy us the time, space, and comfort necessary to enjoy the really important and valuable things. Unfortunately, too often, these things possess us instead of us possessing them.

"When you look back over the days of your life, you will understand that the most valuable things are the love of a child, the respect of your friends and neighbors, and the health and wisdom to enjoy the life that is going on all around you. Wealth and possessions have never made you happy in the past, but too many of us waste more days of our lives to obtain still more possessions that do little more than clutter our lives.

"You have everything you need in order to be joyful, happy, and satisfied. Happiness is a state of mind, not a degree of wealth. Wealth will not make you happy, nor—in the final analysis—will poverty. There is nothing particularly noble or endearing about being poor. When you understand wealth, you will understand that wealth is a direct reflection of the amount of service that we provide to those around us. The more service you provide, the more wealth you will have; but the wealth, itself, will not make you nearly as happy as will the service to those around you.

"If you are not happy today, nothing external will provide the joy you seek. Happiness requires a change of mind. My friends, you change your life when you change your mind.

"These are the things I would have you know this day."

The old man looked again across the huge crowd and seemed to convey love and respect to every individual who was present. Then, he bowed reverently, turned, and walked from the platform. The crowd remained silent for a long time and then began to disperse one or two at a time until just the Keeper of the Flame and I remained.

He spoke. "This society is far advanced from others of its kind during this time. It is even far advanced from civilizations that will develop in the coming centuries. It is not because they have a mighty army or great natural resources or a beautiful city. It is because they have a hunger and a reverence for learning.

"The potential for any society, as well as any individual, can be determined by the premium that is placed upon wisdom and learning. Education is a timeless commodity that serves individuals and societies. People of learning tend to develop quickly. They tend to focus on higher, loftier pursuits. The more a society is educated, the less likely they are to be bogged down in hatred, mistrust or bigotry.

"Seeking brings learning which brings wisdom which results in human advances which creates still more seeking. The educational process develops into a positive upward spiral.

"If you want to predict how well a community will grow, you need not look to the marketplace or the military or even the arts. The greatest predictor will be the schools and the libraries.

"The reverence a society holds for learned individuals is a prime indicator of their future. Great societies seek wisdom and honor the wise among them—even the wise individuals with whom some members of the society disagree. Learned people can disagree, but disagreeable people will never learn."

CHAPTER SEVENTEEN
LIFE AND DEATH

A spark can either light the way or kindle into a funeral pyre.

The burning, blistering sand stretched from horizon to horizon. It softly undulated across the landscape as a flaming serpent on a long, arduous journey. The sun bore down from the brassy sky as a reminder that everything here was permeated with heat and death.

In the middle of this barren wasteland, a spindly metal tower had been erected. It stood alone as if the child of a vast giant had built it and then left his plaything behind. Atop the tower perched a shining, metal, oblong sphere. It waited ominously like some kind of strange and dangerous egg.

The Keeper of the Flame and I were suspended at the edge of this stark world, observing everything below. My attention was repeatedly drawn to the tower as there was no sign of life or habitation anywhere in view.

My companion began to speak. "We are here at this time and place to witness the end of one world and the beginning of another. Everything that existed before this time lived with a certain set of rules and laws in the universe. Everything that will exist from this point forward will come to understand that here, today, the rules will now and forevermore be changed."

As I looked toward the Keeper of the Flame to try and discern some meaning from his cryptic words, there was a flash of light and a sound that vanquished everything my senses could perceive.

All was light, sound, heat, and intensity. It could have lasted for a second or a century. There was no point of perspective that I could relate to. Eventually, I realized that the light was gone, and my eyes began to function again. The sound echoed away, and my ears strained to hear anything that might be left.

I could only stare at the Keeper of the Flame with what must have been an expression of total dumbfounded shock and horror as I sought for some explanation.

He spoke. "A new age has just dawned for all of humanity. The world was created with elements made up of individual atoms. These atoms hold the key to everything. Generations of learned people have stacked their knowledge one atop the other until their combined practical understanding of the world's elements and energy culminated in the detonation of the first atomic bomb."

The tower that had been there was simply gone. There was no remnant, scrap, or shred of the structure that had stood there before. The vast desert wasteland that had earlier been in evidence had been destroyed.

When I had first observed the landscape, it had seemed to hold nothing of value or beauty. Now I longed for that view of the golden sand stretching out to meet the sun and sky upon the horizon.

What was left after the explosion was like nothing I had ever seen. The surface of the sand had been superheated and burned until it had congealed into a hellish volcanic wasteland. Waves of jagged shards of glass protruded everywhere as the sand making up the very earth's surface had been transformed and destroyed.

As I was preparing to inquire of my guide to try and gain some level of understanding, we were instantly transported to another place. A formidable naval vessel made its way through the endless ocean waves. Men scurried about its deck with a practiced and precise routine that made me realize they could have no knowledge of the conflagration I had witnessed in the desert.

The Keeper of the Flame answered my unasked question. "The ship you see below you is the messenger of the atomic force you just saw being unleashed. They have been made aware of the events in the desert, and these men are traveling to deliver another atomic bomb to be dropped on unsuspecting people on the other side of the world.

"They do not understand the global or historic impact of what they have done or are preparing to do. They do, however, know and understand that their entire world has been at war for years, and their leaders have chosen an unimaginable violence as a pathway to peace."

I spoke the question that was shouting out from my mind, demanding to be answered. "How can any destruction—the magnitude of what we just saw—be a pathway to peace?"

My guide and mentor answered. "The atoms that make up the elements of every thing and person from the beginning of time until now are neither good nor evil. Atoms have been combined to make spears, knives, guns, as well as food to feed and nourish the hungry, and the scriptures that feed humanity's soul.

"The ability to create brings with it the ability to destroy. And no discovery ever made can be eliminated from the world any more than a bell can be un-rung. This knowledge that has exploded within the known world can never be eliminated. It can only be managed or abused.

"The same spark that you saw light and warm the earliest of your brothers and sisters has now grown to an intensity that can either power or destroy the entire world. We cannot ignore the danger or the potential. He who would choose to remain oblivious to the oncoming winter and fail to make preparations may well perish due to his foolish desire to ignore reality. Understanding should bring respect but not fear. Ignorance can never bring respect and will always deliver fear.

"The ability to communicate with one person allows you to have either an enlightening or confrontational dialogue. The ability to communicate with many can deliver learning, power, and passion or destruction, deceit, and oblivion. This which we have seen today must never be ignored. It, like every other part of the creation, must be understood and dealt with in love and compassion.

"Every element of this earth that has been formed into a person or thing is a part of all we have and all we know. It is to be respected and approached with reverence. Then and only then do we enter into the knowledge that—whether it be the tiniest spark or the fiery explosion of everything—we are all fellow travelers moving into the future together, and we are each and every one ultimately the Keeper of the Flame."

CHAPTER EIGHTEEN
THE END OF THE JOURNEY

*The great journeys of life
end only as a new journey
begins.*

A filmy curtain of fog drifted across the seascape and blurred the edges of the ship delivering its deadly cargo. The fog thickened, and slowly it became the immense sea of clouds that stretched from horizon to horizon. Somehow I knew that the image of life and death hanging in the balance would always be with me, and I knew it would always remain in the hearts, minds, and souls of all humanity for generations to come.

The Keeper of the Flame was silhouetted against the backdrop of the sea of clouds below and the infinite vault of black space above. He stood serenely, holding the earthen vessel containing the eternal glowing flame.

After a long, uncomfortable silence, I finally voiced the question foremost in my mind. "So, where do we go from here?"

Although I still felt the fear born out of the bizarre travels in time and space, I found myself eagerly awaiting our next journey.

The Keeper of the Flame spoke as if he had not heard my question. "You have seen the first ones who captured the flame and how they kept it—along with the wisdom of their people—alive. You have seen the first people to create their own society and culture as they cultivated and grew the food, not only for their bodies, but for their minds and souls You have felt the uncertainty and fragility of standing on the deck of a small, ancient vessel, exploring the immense ocean and the lands beyond. You have seen the ancient cultures of the ones who came before recorded history. You have met the ancient warriors and the great artists from the Far East."

As the Keeper of the Flame reviewed our travels, I experienced each of my journeys in time and space again. It was more vivid than a memory and more real than a dream. Somehow my senses had been heightened. I knew I could never see anything again as simple, mundane, or ordinary.

The Keeper of the Flame continued. "You have been to the immense mountain and met the master who lived there. You have met the great and famous poet as well as the unparalleled but obscure musician. You have been to the monumental library and traveled to the time and place of the printing press that would forever free wisdom from the clutches and control of little men with small minds.

"You have learned the lesson of the marathon in the ancient Olympic games. You met the mountain man and the bear who were both an integral part of their environment. You met the great teacher and observed the results of a people who hunger for learning. And, finally, you experienced the never-ending cycle of the potential for life and death held within every atom."

As the Keeper of the Flame's words flowed from him, they continued to take me back to each time and place in more vivid detail. The experiences had changed me forever. The change was not only in the way I thought but the way I felt and reacted. I knew I could never be the same. The Keeper of the Flame had not only altered what I knew, but had extended my knowledge and understanding far beyond anything I had ever imagined. There is no way to truly understand that which you have not yet experienced, and there is no way to fully experience that which you do not yet understand.

All of these new revelations had not satisfied my growing hunger for wisdom and knowledge. In fact, the hunger was growing stronger, like a tiny spark fanned into a flame and growing into a raging inferno.

I restated my question. "Where do we go from here? What is our next time and place? What more do you have for me to see and hear and know?"

As I looked on, the Keeper of the Flame seemed to become translucent. He was there but more distant. His voice sounded hollow.

"Since the beginning of time, men and women have been molded by their surroundings. A person can only be judged against the backdrop of his or her time and place. He who would be known as a barbarian in one time would be a heroic figure in another. He who would be learned centuries ago would be dwarfed by the accumulated knowledge of the passage of time.

"Men and women have always fantasized about life in another time and place. It is somehow more romantic or exciting to think of living elsewhere. While there is much to be learned from all peoples of all times and places, one must focus on the here and now. One must learn to live in the moment, because every moment of every day of every life holds within it the key to human greatness which is the ability to exercise your right to choose and change your life by simply changing your mind. He who would seek the greatness in his own time and place would be a master throughout all of history."

The Keeper of the Flame stared at me with those all-knowing, burning eyes. While his gaze grew sharper, the rest of him seemed to blur and fade. The flame within the earthen vessel he held before him grew dim. His voice was an echo.

"Next, you will experience all of the sights, sounds, textures, and tastes of the most exciting, fulfilling, and fascinating time and place the world has ever known. You will be able to gain more wisdom and knowledge from this journey than any that has gone before. All the lessons you have learned from the beginning of time have prepared you to fully experience this most exciting point in history."

The bottom dropped out of the universe. I was falling farther and faster than I would have thought possible. I had no point of reference. Everything was simply blackness rushing past me. I looked up and discovered to my horror that even the Keeper of the Flame was gone. I was alone in a universe of nothingness.

Then, everything exploded, and I lay motionless for what could have been minutes or eternity. Slowly, almost imperceptibly, my senses returned to me one at a time. I could hear water rushing toward me and crashing somewhere below. I could feel the cold, damp, unforgiving granite beneath me. I could smell and begin to taste the sea air. As my eyes opened, the scene swam into focus.

I was perched high atop the boulder where I had first met the Keeper of the Flame. I was facing out to sea and could just make out the last glow of color in the western sky. I looked all about me but discovered I was totally alone.

I began to wonder what was real and what was imagined. My mind told me that everything I had experienced couldn't be real, but my soul told me that the wisdom I now held couldn't be anything but real. I wondered how many days, months, or years I had been gone from this place.

I slowly stood to my feet and made my way back to the beach. As I began walking back the way I had come a lifetime ago, I felt the warm waves roll up onto the sand and caress my feet. I looked down to discover a single set of footprints in the sand that were being slowly eroded by the encroaching inevitability of the tide. It seemed impossible but inescapable that these were my footprints and could have only been made mere moments before. Everywhere I had been and everything I had experienced since the beginning of time had happened in the blink of an eye.

Although I have returned to that very spot at the ocean's shore many times in the ensuing years, the Keeper of the Flame has never returned to me. But maybe in the most important and significant ways, he has never left me.

I have had a good life. I have tasted the depths of the bitterness and the heights of the sweetness that this world has to offer. I have seen men at their best and at their worst and have come to understand the wisdom that the Keeper of the Flame shared with me. I know that the time and place where each of us live offers the best of everything.

NOTES